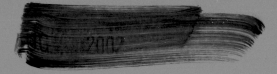

WHAT DO YOU KNOW ABOUT

PEOPLE WITH
DISABILITIES

PETE SANDERS and STEVE MYERS

COPPER BEECH BOOKS

BROOKFIELD, CONNECTICUT

Designed and produced by
Aladdin Books Ltd
28 Percy Street
London W1P 0LD

First published
in the United States in 1998 by
Copper Beech Books,
an imprint of
The Millbrook Press
2 Old New Milford Road
Brookfield, Connecticut 06804

Printed in Belgium

Design   David West
                    Children's
                    Book Design
Editor   Sarah Levete
Illustrator   Mike Lacey
Picture Research   Brooks Krikler
                    Research

Library of Congress
Cataloging-in-Publication Data
Sanders, Pete.
People with disabilities / Pete Sanders and
Steve Myers ; illustrated by Mike Lacey.
p. cm. — (What do you know about)
Includes index.
Summary: Discusses what it means to have a
physical impairment or learning disability and
the effects of such challenges on the disabled
person and those around him.
ISBN 0-7613-0803-2 (lib. bdg.)
1. Handicapped—Juvenile literature.
[1. Handicapped.] I. Myers, Steve. II. Lacey,
Mike, ill. III. Title. IV. Series: Sanders, Pete.
What do you know about.
HV1568.S264 1998   97-41645
362.4—dc21   CIP AC

5 4 3 2 1

CONTENTS

HOW TO USE THIS BOOK

The books in this series are intended to help young people to understand more about issues that may affect their lives.

Each book can be read by a child alone, or together with a parent, teacher, or helper. Issues raised in the storyline are further discussed in the accompanying text, so that there is an opportunity to talk through ideas as they come up.

At the end of the book there is a section called "What Can We Do?" This gives practical ideas which will be useful for both young people and adults. Organizations and helplines are also listed, to provide the reader with additional sources of information and support.

INTRODUCTION

THERE ARE MILLIONS OF PEOPLE IN THE WORLD WITH SOME FORM OF DISABILITY.

For most this will be a physical impairment or a learning difficulty.
This book will help you to understand what it means to have a physical impairment or learning difficulty and the disabling effect that this can have on a person's life. It will help you to be aware of the social and personal issues which challenge a person with a disability. Each chapter introduces a different aspect of the subject, illustrated by a continuing storyline. The characters in the story have to deal with situations which many people have experienced. After each episode, we stop and look at the issues raised and broaden the discussion. By the end, you will know more about disability and some of the physical, emotional, and social difficulties disabled people may face.

WHAT IS A DISABILITY?

A DISABILITY IS OFTEN DESCRIBED AS AN IMPAIRMENT OR MEDICAL CONDITION WHICH PREVENTS SOMEONE FROM PERFORMING A SPECIFIC TASK OR FUNCTION.

However, many people consider that it is not the impairment itself which is disabling, but the fact that society often limits the opportunities that are available to disabled people. An impairment may be caused by the loss of part or all of a limb, or by an organ or mechanism of the body not working properly. A physical impairment affects the working of the body. A learning impairment or difficulty restricts a person's mental development. People become disabled when, as a result of their impairment, they are faced with physical and social barriers which make it difficult for them to participate fully within the community.

Wheelchair users may be "disabled" by an environment which denies them access to places simply because they are not accessible to wheelchair users.

▽ It was Friday evening. Paul Ryan and his friends were on their way home from school.

HEY, LAUREN, ISN'T THAT SYLVIE AND YOUR MOM?

THEY MUST HAVE BEEN SHOPPING FOR A NEW DRESS FOR SYLVIE. HER ACTING GROUP'S DOING A SHOW TONIGHT. SHE'S BEEN EXCITED ABOUT IT ALL WEEK.

HI, SYLVIE. LAUREN SAYS YOU'RE GOING TO BE IN A SHOW TONIGHT. IS THAT AT SCHOOL?

YES. YOU CAN COME. I'M GOING TO DANCE. I LIKE DANCING. ANGELA CAN COME, CAN'T SHE?

HEY PAUL, FIONA - LOOK AT THE WEIRDO. DON'T GET TOO CLOSE.

IF SHE WANTS TO. LET'S SEE WHAT YOU'VE BOUGHT, THEN.

△ Sylvie held up her dress. Phil nudged Gino and started to giggle.

▽ Lauren, Sylvie, and their mom left. The others started to argue with Phil.

PHIL WAS ONLY JOKING. I THINK LAUREN WAS EMBARRASSED. I WOULDN'T LIKE TO HAVE A SISTER LIKE THAT, WOULD YOU, MICK?

WHY NOT? SHE'S REALLY NICE. WHAT PAUL AND PHIL SAID WAS JUST CRUEL.

PEOPLE LIKE THAT GIVE ME THE CREEPS.

THAT'S MY SISTER YOU'RE TALKING ABOUT. SHE'S NOT WEIRD. SHE JUST HAS DOWN'S SYNDROME.

I DIDN'T MEAN ANYTHING. I WOULDN'T HAVE SAID ANYTHING IF I'D KNOWN IT WAS YOUR SISTER.

△ Lauren told Phil that wasn't the point. He and Paul would still have thought those things.

WHAT SORT OF DANCING DO YOU THINK SHE DOES? I BET SHE LOOKS RIDICULOUS.

I CAN HEAR, YOU KNOW. I'M A BETTER DANCER THAN YOU. I DON'T LIKE YOU VERY MUCH.

SHE IS GOOD. COME ALONG, PHIL. YOU MIGHT LEARN SOMETHING.

△ Phil started to make fun of Sylvie.

▽ On the way home, Lauren told her mom what Phil had said.

IT'S NOT FAIR, MOM. WHY DO THEY SAY THINGS LIKE THAT?

I DON'T KNOW, DARLING. I THINK THEY'RE JUST AFRAID BECAUSE SYLVIE'S DIFFERENT FROM THEM. IF THEY TOOK TIME TO GET TO KNOW HER, THEY'D REALIZE HOW WRONG THEY ARE.

I DON'T LIKE PEOPLE CALLING ME NAMES. THERE'S LOTS OF THINGS I CAN DO.

It is important to think carefully about the way we describe others.

Many of the slang words which have been used to describe disabled people are very offensive. Some words can be upsetting, even when the speaker doesn't mean to be insulting. People will sometimes tell you "I was only joking" or "I didn't mean it." This is no excuse. Use of this kind of language stops you from viewing people as individuals.

Sylvie behaves differently from some of Paul's friends.

Some disabilities are more visible than others. This can affect the way in which we react to a person. Unfortunately, many people focus on the impairment rather than on the person. It is also important to be aware of the challenges facing someone whose disability is not immediately obvious. We all have different strengths and abilities, some visible and some hidden.

Phil has made up his mind that Sylvie would look ridiculous dancing.

He has come to this conclusion even though he knows nothing about Sylvie nor about Down's Syndrome. He is making assumptions and confusing disability with inability. Although an impairment may prevent some people from doing certain things, in many cases it doesn't. It might just mean a person learning a different way of doing something, and of others accepting this. This is one reason why many people dislike the word "disabled." They prefer the term "person with disability."

BECOMING DISABLED

THERE ARE ALL KINDS OF IMPAIRMENTS WHICH MAKE PEOPLE DISABLED.

Each person is unique. People with the same kind of impairment may be affected in different ways and to varying degrees.

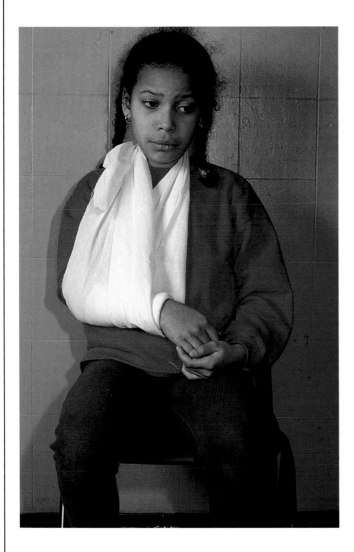

Some conditions which cause an impairment are passed down from parent to child. These are genetic or hereditary conditions. Others may be caused by the body not growing properly, or by disease. Many are the result of accidents. Most disabilities are permanent, although their nature as well as the needs of the disabled person may change. For instance, someone who has had a stroke may at first be seriously disabled. This may improve in time. With specialized support, someone with a learning disability is often able to overcome some of his or her difficulties. The majority of disabled people are not ill, although some will have medical conditions which do affect their health.

A broken bone can make a person temporarily incapable of doing certain things. But this is very different from being permanently disabled.

▽ The following Monday, Angela and Lauren were discussing Sylvie's show.

I'M GLAD I WENT. SYLVIE WAS GREAT.

SHE'S TALKED ABOUT NOTHING ELSE ALL WEEKEND. FIONA, WHAT'S WRONG?

HAVE YOU HEARD ABOUT PAUL? APPARENTLY, HE WAS KNOCKED DOWN ON SATURDAY NIGHT. MICK SAYS HE'S IN A REALLY BAD WAY.

▽ Paul was in the hospital. His back had been injured in the accident.

PAUL'S CONDITION IS NOT GOOD. THE DAMAGE TO HIS SPINE IS VERY SERIOUS. IT WILL BE SOME TIME BEFORE WE CAN BE CERTAIN, BUT YOU SHOULD BE PREPARED FOR THE POSSIBILITY THAT HE MAY BE PARALYZED.

WHY HIM? HOW WILL WE TELL HIM?

WE'LL FIND A WAY. WHEN WILL YOU KNOW FOR SURE, DOCTOR?

IN A FEW WEEKS. WE NEED TO WAIT FOR SOME OF THE INITIAL SHOCK OF HIS INJURIES TO WEAR OFF, BEFORE WE CAN ASSESS HIM PROPERLY.

IT'S SO HARD TO TAKE IN. THREE DAYS AGO, HE WAS RUNNING TO MEET HIS FRIENDS AND NOW THIS.

▽ One evening, Angela and Lauren bumped into Paul's brother.

NEIL, I'M SO SORRY ABOUT PAUL. HOW IS HE?

WELL, I DON'T THINK IT'S REALLY SUNK IN YET. HE'S A BIT DEPRESSED, BUT HE'LL BE OKAY. YOU CAN VISIT HIM IF YOU WANT. HE'D REALLY LIKE THAT.

▽ Two months later, the doctor confirmed that Paul was paralyzed from the waist down.

OF COURSE WE WILL.

WE WENT TO SEE PAUL LAST NIGHT. HE'S STILL IN BED, BUT HE SEEMS TO BE ALL RIGHT. I DON'T THINK I'D BE AS CHEERFUL IF I WAS HIM.

WHAT DO YOU WANT HIM TO DO? CRY ALL THE TIME?

HE'LL HAVE TO USE A WHEEL-CHAIR. LOTS OF PEOPLE DO. MY DAD'S BOSS USES ONE.

YOU'RE JOKING! THAT MUST BE STRANGE FOR YOUR DAD.

◁ Lauren said it was attitudes like his that created problems for disabled people.

LAUREN DIDN'T MEAN THAT, MICK. BUT YOU CAN'T SAY IT'S NOT GOING TO BE A PROBLEM FOR HIM. HE'S GOING TO BE DISABLED FOR LIFE.

WHY? WHY SHOULDN'T HE HAVE A DISABLED BOSS?

YOU'RE SUCH A PAIN, PHIL. SYLVIE'S RIGHT ABOUT YOU. YOU JUST THINK THAT BECAUSE SOMEONE'S DISABLED, THEY CAN'T DO ANYTHING.

General information about some of the most common medical conditions which can cause physical or mental impairment is given below. It is important to remember that the degree to which each person's life is affected will depend on the individual, his or her personal circumstances, and the social conditions he or she faces.

Autism • Research suggests that this is a physical problem that affects the parts of the brain which process language and information received from the senses • May be caused by a chemical imbalance in the brain • Affects a person's communication and development skills.

Brain Damage • The brain is responsible for controlling everything that happens to the body • Damage, either before birth or as a result of an accident, can lead to a variety of impairments, both physical and mental, depending on which part of the brain is affected, and how badly.

Cerebral Palsy • Caused by brain damage occurring at birth or in young children • May result in problems of movement, sensory impairment, learning difficulties, or epilepsy • Effects vary from an unsteady walk to multiple disabilities.

Cystic Fibrosis • Passed on genetically • Causes the mucus in the body to thicken, blocking the air passages, making breathing difficult • People with cystic fibrosis will cough frequently, which helps to clear the lungs. They may need to do special exercises and take plenty of rest breaks • Exercise and prescription drugs can help control the condition.

Down's Syndrome • Caused by an irregularity in the cells of a baby during pregnancy • People with Down's Syndrome may have unusual facial features and have specific physical or mental impairments, such as poor hearing or vision and difficulty learning.

Epilepsy • A disorder of the nervous system, which causes people to have seizures or fits which may take the form of a sudden loss of consciousness or uncontrollable movements • The frequency and length of these attacks varies from person to person, and they may be brought on by specific factors, such as flashing lights.

Multiple Sclerosis • A disease of the central nervous system, which causes damage to the protective covering around nerves • The signals from nerves to the brain and spine are not transmitted properly, resulting in a range of physical problems, from difficulty in moving to visual impairment.

Muscular Dystrophy • An inherited condition which becomes more severe as a child grows older • Causes a gradual breakdown of the muscle fibers, leading to a weakening of all the muscles • A person may eventually need to use a wheelchair or a brace to keep the spine straight.

Sensory Impairments • Aural impairment is the term to describe any kind of hearing problem, from being "hard of hearing" to total deafness • Visual impairment refers to a serious loss of sight that cannot be corrected • Speech or language impairment means difficulty with speech • Sensory impairments may be due to a problem before birth, or may be a result of disease or damage to the particular part of the body.

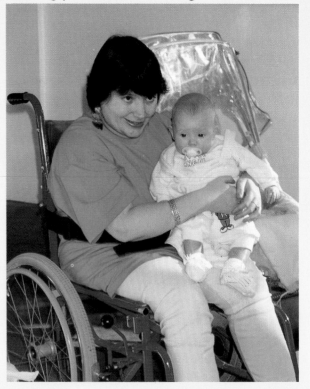

Spina Bifida • A condition which means that the bones in the spine are incomplete • Usually results in some paralysis, depending on the severity of the damage to the spine • A person with spina bifida may have no feeling in parts of their body below the point at which the damage to their spine has occurred.

Spinal Injury • An inability to move a particular part of the body • May occur for a variety of reasons, usually through some form of damage to the spinal cord, either through disease or accident • The two most commonly heard words used to describe the different forms of paralysis are: paraplegia – paralysis affecting the legs only; and quadriplegia – where all limbs are affected.

Stroke • A sudden loss of brain function, caused by a brief interference to the brain's blood supply • Can be fatal, but many people make good recoveries • Some people may be left with permanent physical impairment such as loss of speech or paralysis of part of the body.

REACTIONS TO DISABILITY

A PERSON'S REACTION TO A DISABILITY DEPENDS ON SEVERAL FACTORS.

These include the individual's personality, his or her lifestyle, the cause and severity of the impairment, and the support he or she receives from others.

Many non-disabled people assume that having a disability can only be a negative experience. But this is not always so. Sudden impairment, perhaps as the result of an accident, may at first leave both the disabled person and those to whom he or she is close with a sense of loss or hopelessness. However, many people say that once they have come to terms with their feelings, being disabled has made them aware of different priorities and values in life. Many people with a disability will feel anger not so much at their impairment but at the way in which society and their environment limits the opportunities available to them.

The effect of disability can also depend on the level of love, security, and support a person receives from other people.

▽ It was six months later. Mick, Gino, and Fiona had gone to see Paul at home.

SO WHEN ARE YOU COMING BACK TO SCHOOL, PAUL?

WHY? IT DOESN'T RUN ON GAS, DOES IT?

HOW CAN YOU TWO JOKE? I THINK YOU'RE BEING REALLY BRAVE, PAUL.

I DON'T KNOW. THERE'S A PROBLEM ABOUT ME GOING BACK BECAUSE OF ACCESS. THE BUILDING HASN'T BEEN DESIGNED FOR WHEELCHAIRS YET. I MAY NEED A HELPER TO GET AROUND THE SCHOOL. THEY EVEN THINK THE WHEELCHAIR MAY BE A FIRE RISK!

DON'T YOU START. MY GRANDMA WAS HERE YESTERDAY. SHE KEEPS HUGGING ME AND TELLING ME HOW WELL I'M TAKING IT.

BUT YOU ARE. I CAN'T IMAGINE HOW I'D FEEL. I'D BE SO ANGRY.

WHO SAYS I'M NOT ANGRY? BUT I CAN HARDLY GO AROUND SCREAMING AT EVERYONE ALL THE TIME. I'VE HAD A LOT OF TIME TO THINK ABOUT THINGS.

IT MUST TAKE SOME GETTING USED TO.

SURE, BUT I REALIZED IT WASN'T THE END OF EVERYTHING. I'VE MET LOADS OF OTHER PEOPLE WITH ALL DIFFERENT DISABILITIES. THEY'RE ALL JUST ORDINARY PEOPLE, GETTING ON WITH THEIR LIVES.

△ Paul said many people didn't feel that their disability got in the way of their lives.

HOW CAN THAT BE? I DON'T THINK I'D THINK THAT.

IS THAT HOW YOU FEEL?

PARTLY. BUT MOSTLY IT'S NOT THE THINGS I CAN'T DO BECAUSE I'M PARALYZED, BUT THE THINGS I'M STOPPED FROM DOING. I CAN WHEEL MYSELF TO THE CORNER STORE, BUT I CAN'T GO IN IF THERE'S A STEP.

I DON'T KNOW YET. MY LIFE'S CERTAINLY CHANGED. IT DEPENDS ON YOUR SITUATION, I SUPPOSE. I KNOW I'M STILL ME. MOST OF THE TIME I JUST FEEL FRUSTRATED.

YOU MEAN AT NOT BEING ABLE TO DO THINGS - LIKE PLAY FOOTBALL?

△ Paul said lots of the things he had taken for granted before were a real issue now.

▽ A few days later, Lauren had arranged to take Sylvie swimming. Sylvie suddenly changed her mind.

DON'T WANT TO GO ANYMORE. I WON'T GO AND YOU CAN'T MAKE ME.

COME ON, SYLVIE - YOU WERE LOOKING FORWARD TO IT YESTERDAY. I'M SICK OF YOU DOING THIS. OH, DO WHAT YOU WANT - BUT DON'T EXPECT ME TO GO SWIMMING WITH YOU AGAIN.

DAD, DON'T YOU EVER WISH THAT SYLVIE DIDN'T HAVE DOWN'S SYNDROME?

I DID FOR A WHILE, JUST AFTER SHE WAS BORN. YOUR MOM AND I DIDN'T KNOW HOW WE'D COPE. I MEAN, YOU DON'T THINK YOUR CHILD IS GOING TO BE DISABLED AND WE KNEW IT WOULD MEAN CHANGES IN OUR LIVES.

I LOVE HER, TOO. I JUST NEED TO HAVE SOME SPACE TO MYSELF SOMETIMES, AND IT SEEMS LIKE SYLVIE'S ALWAYS AROUND.

THAT'S BECAUSE SHE'S YOUR SISTER. AND ALL SISTERS GET ON EACH OTHER'S NERVES NOW AND AGAIN. WHY DON'T YOU GO DOWNSTAIRS AND SEE HER?

▽ Lauren ran up to her room. Lauren's dad came up a little while later and asked what had happened.

I'M SORRY IF I UPSET HER. I JUST FEEL SO ANGRY WITH HER SOMETIMES. IT'S LIKE WE'VE ALL GOT TO GO ALONG WITH WHAT SYLVIE WANTS, AND IT'S NOT FAIR.

I KNOW SHE CAN BE DEMANDING. WHEN SHE GETS AN IDEA INTO HER HEAD, IT'S HARD TO MAKE HER THINK OF ANYTHING ELSE.

I REALIZED I WASN'T THINKING ABOUT SYLVIE AS A PERSON. DOWN'S SYNDROME IS ONLY PART OF WHO SYLVIE IS. PEOPLE FORGET THAT SOMETIMES. SHE'S A WONDERFUL DAUGHTER AND A SISTER WHO LOVES YOU VERY MUCH. I WOULDN'T CHANGE EITHER OF YOU FOR THE WORLD.

I DON'T LIKE IT WHEN YOU SHOUT AT ME.

I'M SORRY, SYLVIE. I SHOULDN'T HAVE SNAPPED AT YOU. ARE WE STILL FRIENDS?

△ Sylvie smiled and hugged her sister.

Paul is gradually coming to terms with his disability and the changes it will mean to his life.

It can often be difficult to adapt to change, and there may be many uncomfortable feelings to face. Adjusting to having a disability does not mean you have to accept everything about your situation. For instance, while there may be very little that can be done about your impairment, there is no reason why you cannot challenge the unnecessary barriers and unhelpful attitudes you may have to face.

Fiona thinks that Paul is being brave.

Disabled people are frequently faced with difficulties and obstacles which they have no choice but to try to overcome, simply to survive. This can take more hard work than bravery. Although she means well, Fiona's attitude implies that a disabled person will only regret his or her condition, rather than coming to terms with it and living life to the fullest.

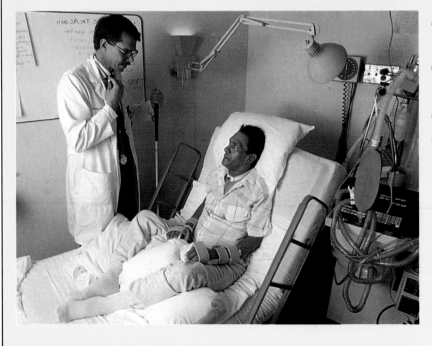

Many assumptions are made about the ability of a disabled person.

People often offer assistance, without thinking whether that is appropriate to the individual. Just because a person may take longer to do something, or may need special equipment to help them, this does not mean others should take over. But if something takes a long time or is very difficult, a disabled person may prefer to ask someone else to do it.

OTHER PEOPLE'S ATTITUDES

DISABLED PEOPLE HAVE TO DEAL NOT ONLY WITH THEIR OWN IMPAIRMENT BUT ALSO WITH THE ATTITUDES OF OTHER PEOPLE TOWARD DISABILITY.

Some of these attitudes may be very hostile. Other people may feel that because the issues of disability don't concern them directly, they do not need to address them.

Historically, those with certain disabilities were poorly treated. A lack of medical expertise meant that there were no treatments available for particular conditions. A lack of understanding led many doctors to recommend that people with disabilities should be removed from society. Today such misguided views have largely been replaced by a fuller understanding of the nature of all disabilities. However, in some cases disabled people are now viewed as needing only sympathy and pity. Such attitudes do little to change the way in which disability is treated in society.

Until the early-to mid-twentieth century, thousands of disabled people, particularly those with a learning disability, were locked away in institutions.

▽ It took another month of negotiation with the principal before Paul was able to go back to school.

WHY SHOULD HE GET SPECIAL TREATMENT JUST BECAUSE HE'S IN THAT THING?

I KNOW. IT'S NOT FAIR TO THE REST OF US.

WHAT DIFFERENCE DOES IT MAKE TO YOU? I'VE AS MUCH RIGHT TO BE HERE AS ANYONE.

PEOPLE ARE STRANGE. SOME ARE FINE, BUT OTHERS EITHER GET REALLY EMBARRASSED OR TALK TO ME LIKE I'M FOUR YEARS OLD. OR ELSE THEY DON'T TALK TO ME AT ALL.

▽ At break time, Lauren talked to Paul in the playground.

DON'T WORRY ABOUT PHIL. ALL HE THINKS ABOUT IS HIMSELF.

IT'S NOT AS IF I LIKE BEING HAULED UP AND DOWN STAIRS. YOU KNOW, PHIL'S REALLY CHANGED. THE OTHER DAY HE EVEN CROSSED THE ROAD TO AVOID ME. AND I THOUGHT WE WERE FRIENDS.

▽ A month later, Angela and Fiona had gone to Lauren's house.

△ Paul said he was tired of being treated like an inconvenience.

▽ Angela said she thought programs like that did a lot of good.

WHAT'S THE MATTER, SYLVIE?

IT'S A SPECIAL CHARITY PROGRAM. BUT I DON'T LIKE THOSE. THEY SHOULDN'T DO THAT.

SYLVIE DOESN'T LIKE THE WAY THEY SHOW DISABLED PEOPLE ON THOSE KIND OF TELETHON EVENTS. AND NEITHER DO I. I THINK THAT SOMETIMES THEY CAN MAKE PEOPLE LOOK AS IF THEY ARE JUST HELPLESS VICTIMS, NEEDING ONLY SYMPATHY AND PITY.

I KNOW THEY RAISE A LOT OF MONEY. BUT THERE ARE LOTS OF PEOPLE WHO BELIEVE THAT DISABLED PEOPLE SHOULDN'T HAVE TO DEPEND ON CHARITY.

DOES IT MATTER HOW THE MONEY IS RAISED?

I THINK IT DOES. I KNOW SOME PEOPLE WHO SAY THAT THEY DON'T WANT CHARITY. BUT I KNOW MOM AND DAD DON'T AGREE WITH THAT.

THE SCHOOL'S DOING SOMETHING, ISN'T IT?

◁ Lauren said that Sylvie's friends were going to try to protest about the program.

Like Phil, many people's views are based simply on ignorance and prejudice.
To them, difference is something to be feared or disliked. In fact, society thrives on difference. Prejudice and discrimination toward disabled people doesn't just take the form of negative comments. In some countries it can be seen in the way buildings are designed or jobs are advertised.

Whether or not it is intentional, any kind of action or behavior which excludes people purely on the grounds of disability should not be acceptable.

Sylvie is unhappy about the charity appeal.
All charities depend on donations to help their work. But many people think that there should be more support from governments to meet the needs of disabled people, making them less dependent upon charities or handouts from others.

Paul is shocked at some of the reactions to his disability.
Some people experience feelings of uneasiness or embarrassment around a disabled person, especially if he or she behaves in a way which seems unusual – perhaps speaking differently or being unable to control certain body movements. Such reactions can be upsetting to someone who has a disability. It is important to think about why you react in a certain way and to remember how it can make others feel.

PERSONAL ASSISTANCE

SOME PEOPLE WITH A SEVERE IMPAIRMENT OR MEDICAL CONDITION MAY NEED CONSTANT HELP ON A DAY-TO-DAY BASIS.

People who take on this role may be known as "carergivers," though many disabled people prefer the term "assistants" or "enablers." Depending on the situation, support may come from members of the family or from someone employed to carry out certain duties. Personal assistants may perform a number of functions, such as cooking or looking after the children. Sometimes they assist with giving medication or with doing exercises to keep the disabled person's body in shape. It is important to remember that not all disabled people need this help, and we are all dependent to a large extent on other people for our needs.

There is no one type of person who becomes a carergiver. It depends on each individual case. Some are obliged to take on the role – perhaps because it is a loved one who has become disabled. To others it is a job for which they are interviewed and paid. Many carergivers or personal assistants are themselves disabled.

▽ It was school vacation. Paul had gone out shopping with Neil and his mom.

LET ME HELP YOU. IS THIS THE ONE YOU'RE INTERESTED IN?

IT'S THE ONE I'M INTERESTED IN. I AM HERE, YOU KNOW.

PAUL, THERE'S NO NEED TO BE RUDE.

I JUST GET SO ANNOYED SOMETIMES. I WANT TO DO THINGS FOR MYSELF. THEN WHEN I CAN'T, I FEEL LIKE I'M MAKING LOTS OF WORK FOR YOU.

WELL, YOU'RE WRONG. LAST YEAR, WHEN GRANDMA HAD HER STROKE SHE COULDN'T WASH OR FEED HERSELF, OR EVEN SPEAK. YOU SPENT A LOT OF TIME HELPING HER. YOU DIDN'T FEEL SHE WAS A BURDEN, DID YOU?

△ Paul shook his head.

▽ Two weeks later, Gino and Fiona met Angela and Lauren in town.

GOOD TO SEE YOU, LAUREN. YOU'VE NOT BEEN AROUND FOR A WHILE.

SHE'S BEEN ON VACATION.

IT WAS GREAT FUN FOR ALL OF US ALL TO GO AWAY TOGETHER. WE CAN'T ALL GO SOMETIMES, BECAUSE SOME HOTELS WON'T LET SYLVIE STAY THERE, OR GET REALLY FUNNY ABOUT IT.

▽ Paul moved away angrily.

I'M SICK OF IT. I HATE PEOPLE TREATING ME LIKE THAT, AND I HATE HAVING TO RELY ON YOU ALL THE TIME.

I'M YOUR MOTHER, PAUL. THAT'S WHAT I'M HERE FOR! LOOK, I KNOW IT'S NOT EASY. IT'S HARD FOR US, TOO. WE ALL WANT TO DO WHAT'S BEST - NOT JUST FOR YOU, BUT FOR EVERYONE. AND WE DON'T ALWAYS GET IT RIGHT.

OK, THEN. WE ALL RELY ON EACH OTHER, PAUL. PERSONALLY, I'M DEPENDING ON YOU TO TEACH ME THAT NEW COMPUTER PROGRAM, AND IF THAT MEANS HELPING YOU IN AND OUT OF THE CAR, THAT'S FINE. DEAL?

DEAL.

△ They both went back over to join Neil.

THAT'S TERRIBLE.

I KNOW. BUT DAD FOUND THIS COMPANY THAT SPECIALIZES IN VACATIONS FOR THE DISABLED. THEY ARRANGED EVERYTHING. WE HAD A WONDERFUL TIME.

Paul is angry because he needs help to do certain things.

In some cases, a disabled person may require another person to assist with very intimate details of his or her life, such as washing or going to the bathroom. This might make someone feel very embarrassed or frustrated. Learning to adapt to this kind of situation can take time, and will require much understanding between the disabled person and the caregiver.

Helping with some forms of disability can be tiring.

However much they care, some assistants may feel angry or resentful from time to time. Others may feel guilty about having needs of their own. Such feelings are natural, although they may be hard to face up to.

Sylvie and her family have been on a vacation booked through a specialized company.

Many family caregivers decide to give up their own time to assist a disabled relative. This is often due to a lack of funding to enable them to employ help.

Looking after someone on a regular basis can put a strain on both the disabled person and the assistant. Feeling dependent on someone else to do things for you can be difficult to come to terms with. It can be of help to both people to have a break from each other – perhaps by someone else taking over for a while, or by going on vacation separately.

LIVING WITH A DISABILITY·

EVERY PERSON'S WAY OF LIFE IS DIFFERENT, REGARDLESS OF WHETHER OR NOT HE OR SHE HAS A DISABILITY.

The degree to which a disability influences a person's daily life will depend on the nature of the impairment, the person involved, when he or she became disabled, and his or her social and economic situation.

Most disabled people are simply trying to get on with their lives in the same way as everyone else.

If someone is still getting used to having an impairment, it may seem to them as though some of the adjustments they have to make are enormous. With time, however, these may become routine. Some disabled people may experience difficult emotions, particularly when they have not come to terms with their impairment. They may be depressed or resentful at not being able to do the things they could before they became disabled. Some can feel they are being a burden to other people.

Many disabled people may feel frustrated, not so much about their impairment, as about the attitudes of society toward them. There are not always the necessary resources nor the social commitment to enable disabled people to overcome some of the practical challenges of their impairment.

▽ One afternoon a couple of months later, Paul and his friends had decided to go to the movies.

I'M AFRAID YOU CAN'T COME IN THIS WAY, SON. WE DON'T HAVE A CUSTOMER ELEVATOR. IF YOU'D LIKE TO GET YOUR TICKET, I'LL SHOW YOU THE WAY.

YOU GO ON IN. I'LL MEET YOU INSIDE.

▽ The attendant took Paul around to a side entrance.

LOOK, I'M SORRY ABOUT THIS. IT'S JUST THAT IT'S A VERY OLD BUILDING. IT WASN'T REALLY DESIGNED FOR WHEELCHAIRS.

SOME PLACES ARE EASIER THAN OTHERS. IT'S LIKE TRAVELING - SOMETIMES I CAN ONLY GET AROUND IF SOMEONE DRIVES ME.

▽ After the movie, the friends went for a burger.

I NEVER REALIZED HOW MANY THINGS I TOOK FOR GRANTED. I MEAN, I CAN GET INTO ANY BUILDING WITHOUT EVEN HAVING TO THINK ABOUT IT.

I DIDN'T THINK ABOUT IT MYSELF BEFORE. BUT WHAT REALLY GETS ME IS WHEN PLACES THINK THEY'RE DOING YOU A FAVOR OR THEY'RE REALLY WEIRD TOWARD YOU.

IT'S AS IF YOU HAVE TO FEEL GRATEFUL FOR BEING HELPED. IT'S ONE OF THE THINGS WE TALK ABOUT AT THE YOUTH CLUB. WE'RE HAVING A DANCE NEXT WEEK. COME ALONG. IT'LL BE FUN.

△ Paul had been going to the club for two months. It was for both disabled and non-disabled people.

▽ One evening, Lauren and Angela found Sylvie writing in the living room.

WHAT ARE YOU UP TO, SYLVIE?

WE'RE DOING A NEWSLETTER AT SCHOOL. I'M WRITING ABOUT THE ACTING GROUP.

THE SCHOOL SOUNDS REALLY GOOD. DO YOU LIKE IT, SYLVIE?

IT'S OK. I WANTED TO GO TO LAUREN'S SCHOOL, BUT I COULDN'T. THEY SAID I WOULDN'T BE ABLE TO LEARN.

MOM AND DAD TRIED ABOUT FOUR YEARS AGO, BUT THE PRINCIPAL SAID THEY DIDN'T HAVE THE SPECIAL HELP THAT SYLVIE WOULD NEED.

SHE WRITES A LOT FOR THE NEWSLETTERS. SHE SAYS SHE WANTS TO BE AN ACTRESS OR WORK ON A NEWSPAPER WHEN SHE'S OLDER.

△ Lauren said she thought people assumed things about what Sylvie could and couldn't do.

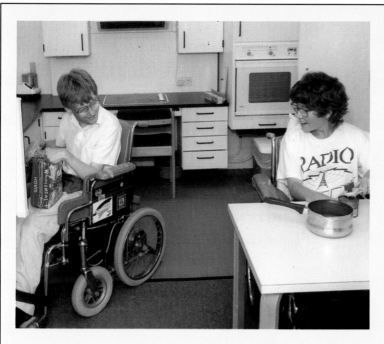

We all want to feel that we are in control of our lives.

Non-disabled people sometimes make assumptions about the extent to which a disabled person can lead an independent life. While some people may want and need help to do certain things, this does not mean they are giving up their independence. Having the right to make decisions about issues which affect their lives is as important for disabled people as it is for others.

Many disabled people face different types of discrimination.

Paul could not enter the movies by the same route as his friends. In most countries, disabled people face similar problems every day. But not all barriers are physical ones. People may be called names and find themselves being stared at; or they may not be considered for jobs because of their impairment. However, many disabled people are involved in movements to challenge such discrimination.

Paul knows that coping with an impairment, and with the daily challenges a disabled person faces, can be emotionally and physically exhausting.

It can be tempting for disabled people to feel like giving up. This is quite natural, since most non-disabled people do not have to deal with the same issues. However, those with a disability do not usually have the choice of giving up. If they did, the quality of their lives would suffer. This is why everyone needs to work together to remove unnecessary barriers.

THE RIGHTS OF DISABLED PEOPLE

EVERYBODY HAS CERTAIN BASIC RIGHTS TO WHICH THEY ARE ENTITLED.

Some countries have legislation designed to protect the rights of disabled people to employment and to stop discrimination. Laws, though, do not always change attitudes.

Today, there is much help available for disabled people and there is an increasing awareness of disability issues. Unfortunately, the amount of support which disabled people receive is not usually enough to cover more than their most basic needs. Some people require specialized care. This may be from residential and day-care centers or educational centers. But these are not always available to everyone who might need them. Although charities provide much support, many people do not agree that the rights and needs of disabled people should be dependent on this.

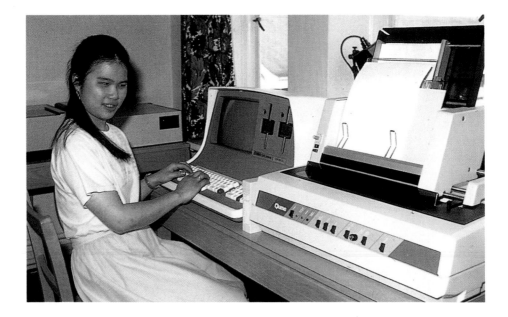

Specialized equipment, which a disabled person may need in order to develop to his or her full potential, is often expensive.

▽ Several of Paul's friends decided to take up his invitation to the dance.

HI, TERRY. THIS IS SYLVIE, MY SISTER.

HELLO. COME ON, LAUREN, LET'S DANCE.

LAUREN, I'M GLAD YOU COULD COME. THIS IS TERRY, A FRIEND OF MINE.

▽ Paul was surprised when Phil turned up ten minutes later with Mick and Angela.

HE TRIED TO BACK OUT WHEN HE FOUND OUT WHERE WE WERE GOING. BUT HE CHANGED HIS MIND WHEN WE TOLD HIM LAUREN WAS GOING TO BE HERE. HE LIKES HER.

BE QUIET, WILL YOU?

I HOPE YOU'RE ALL GOING TO BUY RAFFLE TICKETS.

▽ Paul explained that they needed to buy some new sports equipment.

WHAT DO YOU NEED THAT FOR? WHAT KIND OF SPORTS COULD YOU PLAY?

THE USUAL KIND. I'VE JUST JOINED THE BASKETBALL TEAM, AS A MATTER OF FACT.

WHAT ARE YOU TALKING ABOUT, ANYWAY, PHIL? YOU'RE NO GOOD AT SPORTS. HEY, LOOK AT SYLVIE. SHE'S CERTAINLY HAVING A GOOD TIME!

▽ An hour later, Lauren came over to Paul. He was with Raymond, who ran the club.

WOW! SYLVIE'S WEARING ME OUT. SHE WANTS TO COME BACK NEXT WEEK. SHE'S MADE LOTS OF NEW FRIENDS, AND I'VE JUST LEFT HER DANCING WITH MICK.

I WAS TELLING RAYMOND ABOUT PHIL. IT GETS SO CONFUSING. I DON'T WANT PEOPLE TO TREAT ME AS IF I'M NOT PARALYZED BUT I DON'T WANT IT TO BE ALL THERE IS ABOUT ME.

THAT'S WHY I'M TRYING TO MAKE PEOPLE AWARE OF THE ISSUES AND TO CAMPAIGN FOR THE RIGHTS OF DISABLED PEOPLE.

EVEN WHERE THERE ARE LAWS TO PROVIDE BETTER CONDITIONS FOR DISABLED PEOPLE, IT'S OFTEN DIFFICULT TO MAKE PEOPLE CHANGE THEIR ATTITUDES TOWARD THOSE WHO HAVE ANY DISABILITY.

YEAH, PEOPLE SEEM FRIGHTENED OF ANYBODY WHO'S DIFFERENT.

ALL THE PEOPLE WHO COME TO THE CLUB HAVE DIFFERENT NEEDS AND ABILITIES. BUT WHATEVER A PERSON'S ABILITY, WE ALL DESERVE TO BE TREATED WITH RESPECT AND TO BE GIVEN THE SAME OPPORTUNITIES AS EACH OTHER.

△ Raymond said it was important that everyone should challenge all forms of discrimination.

If a disabled person does need special help, it is essential that this help actually meets the needs of the individual.

It is important to remember that a person's needs may also change gradually, and these may require re-assessment after a period of time. Sometimes, non-disabled people who are providing help may fail to take into account the specific needs of the person.

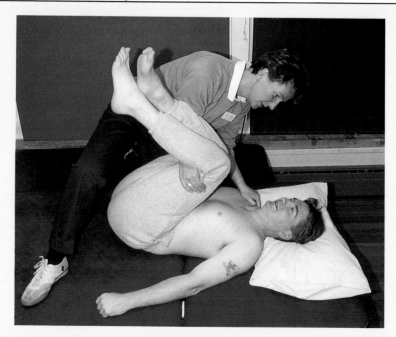

Raymond knows that many non-disabled people take their rights for granted.

Many of the things which are talked about in terms of disabled people's needs would often be considered rights by other people. For instance, most people would expect a public bathroom to be available for them, or to be able to use the bus or enter any public building – or even to go to the school of their choice. But in many countries, these rights are not available to disabled people, simply because of their impairment. However, around the world many disabled people are involved in campaigns to make sure that their rights and needs are met.

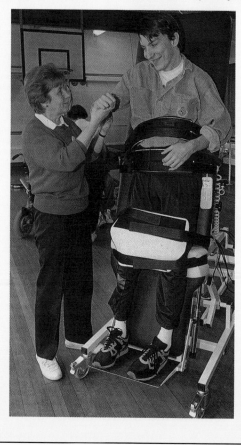

One reason people give for not meeting the needs of disabled people is the expense involved.

Some of the specialized equipment which disabled people use is very expensive. It can also be very costly to make some of the changes necessary to buildings in order to make them accessible to everyone, whatever his or her ability.

Even so, many people believe that the problem is not so much that the money isn't available, but rather that some people do not consider the rights of disabled people to be a priority. They believe that the question of funding has clouded the issue of the basic rights of disabled people.

THINKING DIFFERENTLY.

THE MOST DISABLING FACTOR FOR MANY PEOPLE IS THE WAY IN WHICH DISABILITY IS VIEWED BY SOCIETY.

Many people believe that only a basic change in attitudes and improved physical access for disabled people will guarantee that every disabled person has an equal right within society.

There is a danger that some people with a severe medical condition may be thought of as less worthwhile as a human being than others. But every individual has rights and should be able to make a contribution to the world, however small this may appear to be. People with an impairment do not want to be treated exactly the same as everyone else. But they do want to be seen as equals, however much their impairment makes them physically different from non-disabled people.

A change in attitude may take time, and will probably involve confronting some difficult feelings. Appreciating that we all have different abilities, wants, and needs may be the beginning of the process.

Many disabled and non-disabled people are not as brilliant as the scientist Stephen Hawking. But every person is an individual in his or her own right, whether or not he or she happens to have a disability.

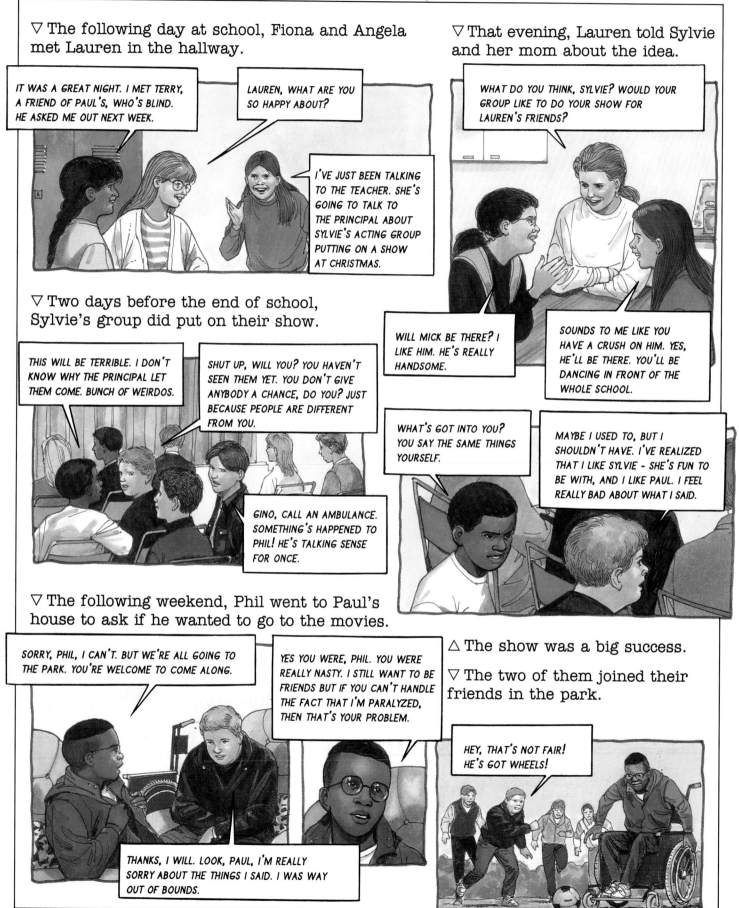

▽ The following day at school, Fiona and Angela met Lauren in the hallway.

IT WAS A GREAT NIGHT. I MET TERRY, A FRIEND OF PAUL'S, WHO'S BLIND. HE ASKED ME OUT NEXT WEEK.

LAUREN, WHAT ARE YOU SO HAPPY ABOUT?

I'VE JUST BEEN TALKING TO THE TEACHER. SHE'S GOING TO TALK TO THE PRINCIPAL ABOUT SYLVIE'S ACTING GROUP PUTTING ON A SHOW AT CHRISTMAS.

▽ Two days before the end of school, Sylvie's group did put on their show.

THIS WILL BE TERRIBLE. I DON'T KNOW WHY THE PRINCIPAL LET THEM COME. BUNCH OF WEIRDOS.

SHUT UP, WILL YOU? YOU HAVEN'T SEEN THEM YET. YOU DON'T GIVE ANYBODY A CHANCE, DO YOU? JUST BECAUSE PEOPLE ARE DIFFERENT FROM YOU.

GINO, CALL AN AMBULANCE. SOMETHING'S HAPPENED TO PHIL! HE'S TALKING SENSE FOR ONCE.

▽ The following weekend, Phil went to Paul's house to ask if he wanted to go to the movies.

SORRY, PHIL, I CAN'T. BUT WE'RE ALL GOING TO THE PARK. YOU'RE WELCOME TO COME ALONG.

YES YOU WERE, PHIL. YOU WERE REALLY NASTY. I STILL WANT TO BE FRIENDS BUT IF YOU CAN'T HANDLE THE FACT THAT I'M PARALYZED, THEN THAT'S YOUR PROBLEM.

THANKS, I WILL. LOOK, PAUL, I'M REALLY SORRY ABOUT THE THINGS I SAID. I WAS WAY OUT OF BOUNDS.

▽ That evening, Lauren told Sylvie and her mom about the idea.

WHAT DO YOU THINK, SYLVIE? WOULD YOUR GROUP LIKE TO DO YOUR SHOW FOR LAUREN'S FRIENDS?

WILL MICK BE THERE? I LIKE HIM. HE'S REALLY HANDSOME.

SOUNDS TO ME LIKE YOU HAVE A CRUSH ON HIM. YES, HE'LL BE THERE. YOU'LL BE DANCING IN FRONT OF THE WHOLE SCHOOL.

WHAT'S GOT INTO YOU? YOU SAY THE SAME THINGS YOURSELF.

MAYBE I USED TO, BUT I SHOULDN'T HAVE. I'VE REALIZED THAT I LIKE SYLVIE - SHE'S FUN TO BE WITH, AND I LIKE PAUL. I FEEL REALLY BAD ABOUT WHAT I SAID.

△ The show was a big success.

▽ The two of them joined their friends in the park.

HEY, THAT'S NOT FAIR! HE'S GOT WHEELS!

Paul goes to the same school as his non-disabled friends.

Many believe that schools should be able to cater to everybody, whether or not they are disabled. Others think that schools which meet the needs of disabled people are preferable. The decision should depend upon each individual case. If both disabled and non-disabled young people mix together on a regular basis, this will help to stop disability being seen as odd or unusual, or as something which does not concern everyone.

Thinking differently has enabled many disabled people to lead independent lives.

People using their feet to write or their mouth to paint, or using a baton attached to their head to punch the keys on a computer, may seem strange to some. But there are no rules which say that just because most people would use their hands, this is the way it has to be done. The sign language of the deaf community is a full and rich form of communication in its own right. By approaching things from a different angle, many solutions to problems have been found.

Phil's prejudice has finally been overcome by listening to others and finding out about disability.

If people try to understand what it means to be disabled, and what they can do to help both practically and emotionally, some of the barriers in attitudes may be broken down. Education can play an important part in this.

WHAT CAN WE DO?

HAVING READ THIS BOOK YOU SHOULD UNDERSTAND MORE ABOUT DISABILITY AND THE EFFECT IT CAN HAVE ON PEOPLE'S LIVES.

You will know that disability is not something to be feared or hidden away, and that disabled people have needs and rights, just like everyone else.

People may have very strong feelings as a result of their own or someone else's disability. It can take a lot of support and understanding from everyone concerned to work them through. Whether or not you have experience of disability, you know that all prejudice and discrimination needs to be challenged.

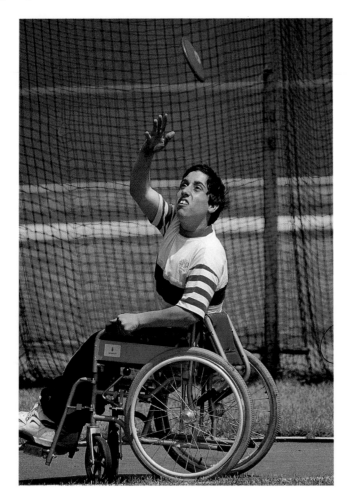

American Disability Association
2121 8th Ave. N., Suite 1623
Birmingham, AL 35203
205-323-0088

National Center For Youth With Disabilities
University of Minnesota Box 721
420 Delaware Street, SE
Minneapolis, MN 55455-0392
612-626-2825

Learning Disabilities Association of America
4156 Library Road
Pittsburgh, PA 15234
412-341-1515

ADULTS CAN HELP TOO, BY RECOGNIZING THAT THEIR OWN ATTITUDES CAN INFLUENCE THE WAY THEIR CHILDREN THINK AND FEEL.

The more young people are given the impression by those close to them that it is acceptable to discriminate against disabled people, the more they are likely to do it.
Adults and children who have read this book together may find it helpful to share their own ideas about or experiences of disability. People who would like more information or require advice or support may be able to obtain help from the organizations listed below.

National Center for Learning Disabilities
318 Park Avenue South, Suite 1401
New York, NY 10016
888-575-7373

HEAR Center
301. E. Del Mar Boulevard
Pasadena, CA 91101
818-796-2016

National Information Center On Deafness
Gallaudet University
800 Florida Avenue, NE
Washington, DC 20002-3695
202-651-5051

American Foundation For the Blind
11 Pennsylvania Plaza,
Suite 300
New York, NY 10001
800-AFB-LINE

National Association For Visually Handicapped
22 W. 21st St.
New York, NY 10010
212-889-3141

Center For Family Support
386 Park Avenue South
New York, NY 10016
212-889-5464

National Information Center For Children And Youth With Disabilities
PO. Box 1492
Washington, DC 20013-1492
202-884-8200

INDEX

Photocredits
All the pictures in this book are by Roger Vlitos apart from pages: cover: Spectrum; 1, 3, 10, 14 top, 18, 20 bottom, 23 top, 26 top and bottom, 29 top, 30: Queen Elizabeth Foundation; 6 bottom, 14 bottom, 27, 29 bottom: Frank Spooner; 17 top, 24: Rex Features; 15: Hulton Deutsch; 4: Marie Helene Bradley; 10 bottom right: Eye Ubiquitous. The publishers wish to acknowledge that all of the photographs in this book have been posed by models.